Are You a Horse?

by Andy Rash

Arthur A. Levine Books • An Imprint of Scholastic Inc.

For Jennifer

Text and illustrations copyright © 2009 by Andy Rash

All rights reserved. Published by Arthur A. Levine Books, an imprint of Scholastic Inc., *Publishers since 1920.* Scholastic and the Lantern Logo are trademarks and/or registered trademarks of Scholastic Inc.

No part of this publication may be reproduced, stored in a retrieval system, or transmitted in any form or by any means, electronic, mechanical, photocopying, recording, or otherwise, without written permission of the publisher. For information regarding permission, write to Scholastic Inc., Attention: Permissions Department, 557 Broadway, New York, NY 10012.

Library of Congress Cataloging-in-Publication Data • Rash, Andy • Are you a horse? / by Andy Rash. — 1st ed • p. cm. • Summary: When Roy gets a saddle for his birthday, he goes in search of a horse. • ISBN-13: 978-0-439-72417-3 (hardcover : alk. paper) • ISBN-10: 0-439-72417-1 • [1. Animals — Fiction. 2. Horses — Fiction.] I. Title • PZ7.R18149Ar 2009 • [E] — dc22 • 2008009972

10 9 8 7 6 5 4 3 2 1 • 09 10 11 12 13 • Printed in Singapore 46 First edition, March 2009 • The art was created using gouache and india ink on Arches watercolor paper. • Book design by Charles Kreloff

Today was Roy's birthday. His friends made a cake and gave him a great big birthday present.

"What's this thing?" Roy asked his friends.

It was a saddle. And, luckily, it came with instructions:

Roy wasn't sure what a horse was, but he couldn't wait to try out his new saddle. So, he went out to find one.

The first thing Roy came to was squeaky and rusty.

"Are you a horse?" he asked.

"Nope, I'm an old wagon," said the wagon. "A horse is a *living thing*."

Next, Roy came to a tall, prickly thing.

"Are you a horse?" he asked.

"I bristle at the thought! I'm a cactus," said the cactus. "A horse is an animal."

After that, Roy saw a wiggly, hissing thing.
"Are you a horse?" he asked.
"A horsssse hasss legsss. I'm a sssnake,"
said the snake.

A skittery, pinchy thing ran sideways in front of Roy.

It had *plenty* of legs.

"Are you a horse?" he asked.

"A horse? I'll pinch you good! A horse is friendly. I'm a crab!" said the crab. "NOW GO AWAY!"

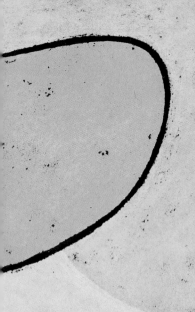

Roy saw a climbing, bug-eyed thing smiling at him.

"Are you a horse?" he asked.

"I can be green or brown or purple," it said.

"But can you be a horse?" Roy asked.

"No. But a horse can't change colors like me. I'm a chameleon," said the chameleon.

Roy came to a tree with a feathered, hooting thing on a branch. It didn't turn green or brown or purple.

"Are you a horse?" he asked.
"Whooo, me? Indeed not!
A horse doesn't lay eggs. I am
an owl," said the owl.

Roy saw a fat, snorting thing rolling around in a mud puddle. He didn't see eggs anywhere.

"Are you a horse?" he asked.

"Oink! Not me! A horse is clean. I'm a muddy, muddy pig!" said the pig.

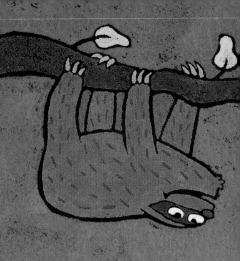

Roy spotted a furry, upside-down thing hanging from a branch. It looked pretty clean.

"Are you a horse?" he asked.

"A . . . horse . . .

is . . . very . . .

very . . . fast.

I . . . am . . . a . . .

sloth,"
said the sloth.

Next, Roy saw a romping, growling thing. It was very fast.

"Are you a horse?" he asked.

"RAAAAR! A horse eats grass. I'm a man-eating lion," said the lion.

"Are you a man?" the lion asked Roy.

"No," said Roy. "I'm a cowboy." And Roy ran away as fast as he could.

After that, Roy came to a quiet,
black-and-white thing eating grass.
"You MUST be a horse!" said Roy.

"I'm not a horse, I'm a zebra," said the zebra.
"A horse doesn't have stripes."
Roy was very upset.

Just as Roy was about to give up, he met one last creature.

It seemed like a lively animal. It had legs and was friendly. It didn't change color or lay eggs.

It was clean and fast. It loved eating grass. And it didn't have stripes. Roy was overjoyed!

"Are YOU a horse?" asked Roy.
"Of course!" said the horse.
"Well, I have a saddle!" said Roy.
"Would you like to go for a ride?"
"Yes!" said the horse.

And so they did.